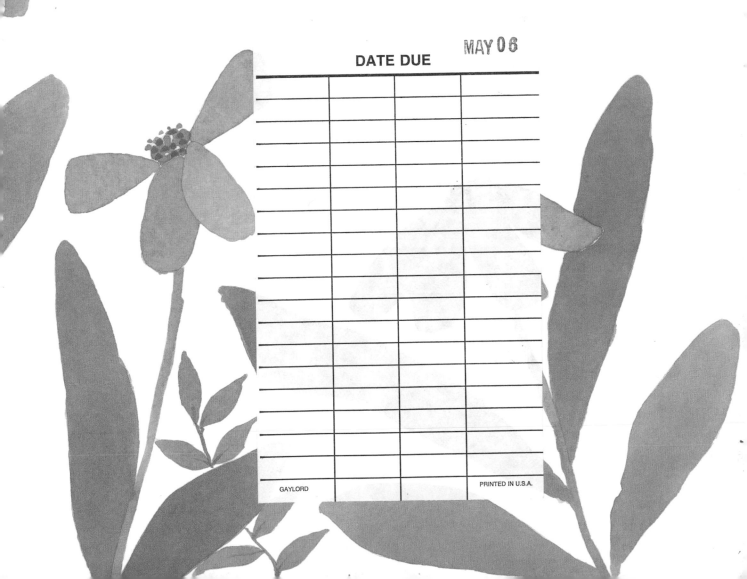

The Bear Hug

Sean Callahan

Illustrated by Laura J. Bryant

Albert Whitman & Company, Morton Grove, Illinois

Library of Congress Cataloging-in-Publication Data

Callahan, Sean, 1965-
The bear hug / by Sean Callahan ; illustrated by Laura J. Bryant.
p. cm.
Summary: Cubby loves spending time with Grandpa Bear,
especially when Grandpa gives him the Bear Hug.
ISBN-13: 978-0-8075-0596-0 (hardcover)
ISBN-10: 0-8075-0596-X (hardcover)
[1. Grandparent and child—Fiction. 2. Bears—Fiction. 3. Hugging—
Fiction.] I. Bryant, Laura J., ill. II. Title.
PZ7.C12974Bea 2006 [E]—dc22 2005024863

The art is rendered in watercolor on paper.
The design is by Laura J. Bryant and Carol Gildar.

For more information about Albert Whitman & Company,
please visit our web site at www.albertwhitman.com.

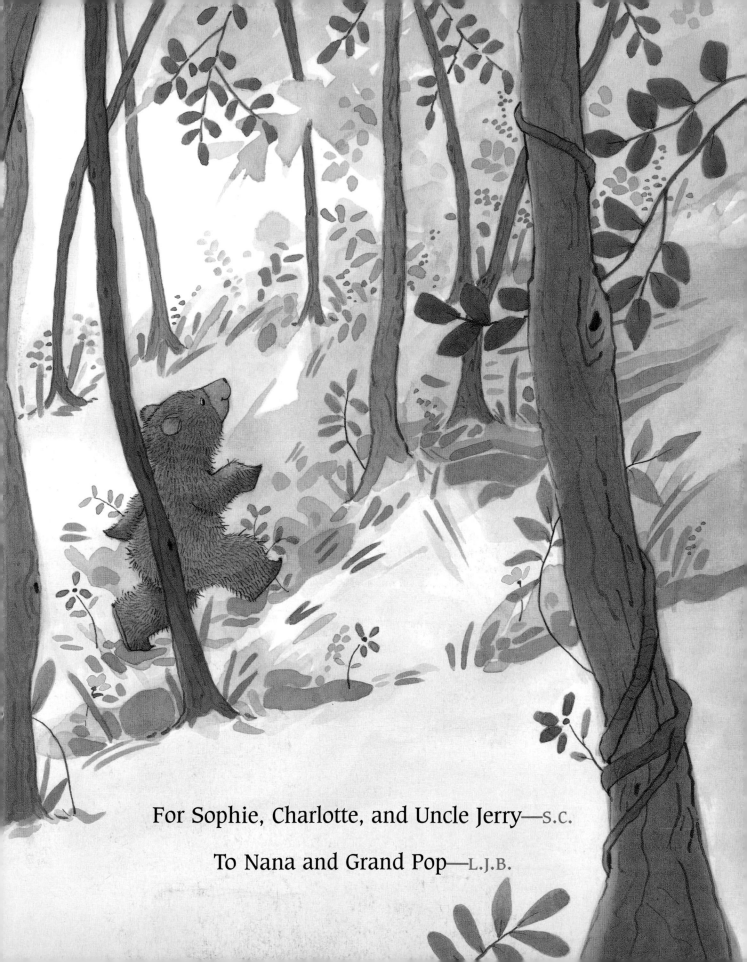

For Sophie, Charlotte, and Uncle Jerry—s.c.

To Nana and Grand Pop—l.j.b.

Every Sunday, Cubby
walked to Grandpa Bear's house.
"Hi, Grandpa Bear," Cubby said.

Grandpa Bear taught little Cubby
how to be a bear.
They always worked on their
growling.

"Grrrrrooooowwwwlllll!"

In the spring, Grandpa Bear
showed off his fishing technique.
"It's all in the wrist,"
Grandpa Bear said.

On summer days, they
splashed at the swimming hole.

"Look out

belooooooooooow!"

Grandpa bellowed.

In the fall, they hunted for
food wherever they could find it.
"Thanks for the bear claw,
Grandpa," Cubby said.

50¢

STRAWBERRY

BLUEBERRY

APPLE

BANANA

DOUGHNUT
SHOP

In the winter, Grandpa Bear
showed Cubby how to hibernate.

"Zzzzzzzzzzzzzzzzzzzzzzzz."

FOOTBALL
Bears in
Play-off Today
Watch the game on
TV tonight

On rainy days, they looked at snapshots of when Grandpa Bear was a cub.

"Wow, that's your grandpa giving *you* the Bear Hug," Cubby said.

The Bear Hug!

Cubby loved the Bear Hug.
It was the best thing about going
to Grandpa Bear's.
"Nobody *ever* gets out of
the Bear Hug," Grandpa Bear
warned Cubby.
"I'm going to get out,"
Cubby vowed.

"Do you give up?" Grandpa Bear asked.
"No," Cubby said. "I'm gonna

wiggle, wiggle, wiggle

my way out!"

"Do you give up?" Grandpa Bear yelled.
"No," Cubby said. "I'm gonna

wriggle, wriggle, wriggle

my way out!"

"Do you give up *now?*" whispered Grandpa.
"No!" Cubby said with a shout. "I'm gonna

giggle,
giggle,
giggle—

'cause I'm

OUT!"

Grandpa Bear moaned. "You got
out of the Bear Hug! How'd you do it?"
"Same way as last week," Cubby
said. "There's really nothing to it!"